Lea is Hungry

by Jay Dale

illustrated by Amanda Gulliver

"I am hungry," said Lea.

"I am hungry, too,"
said Dad.

4

"Here is a sandwich,"
said Dad.

"No," said Lea.
"The sandwich looks too big."

"Here is a banana,"
said Dad.

"No," said Lea.
"The banana looks too big."

"Here is a pear,"
said Dad.

"No," said Lea.
"The pear looks too big."

11

"Look!" said Lea.

"I can see a little carrot."

13

"The little carrot is my lunch."

"The big sandwich
is my lunch," said Dad.